People at Work

Working at a Hospital

by Connor Stratton

FOCUS READERS
SCOUT

www.focusreaders.com

Focus Readers is distributed by North Star Editions:
sales@northstareditions.com | 888-417-0195

Produced for Focus Readers by Red Line Editorial.

Photographs ©: Dragon Images/Shutterstock Images, cover, 1; TheGift777/iStockphoto, 4 (top); Monkey Business Images/Shutterstock Images, 4 (bottom), 16 (bottom right); Yakobchuk Viacheslav/Shutterstock Images, 7; Hispanolistic/iStockphoto, 9 (top); sirtravelalot/Shutterstock Images, 9 (bottom); FatCamera/iStockphoto, 11 (top); all_about_people/Shutterstock Images, 11 (bottom); monkeybusinessimages/iStockphoto, 13; Steve Debenport/iStockphoto, 15 (top), 15 (bottom); Rawpixel.com/Shutterstock Images, 16 (top left); digicomphoto/iStockphoto, 16 (top right); wavebreakmedia/Shutterstock Images, 16 (bottom left)

Library of Congress Cataloging-in-Publication Data
Library of Congress Cataloging-in-Publication Data is available on the Library of Congress website.

ISBN
978-1-64493-015-1 (hardcover)
978-1-64493-094-6 (paperback)
978-1-64493-252-0 (ebook pdf)
978-1-64493-173-8 (hosted ebook)

Printed in the United States of America
Mankato, MN
012020

About the Author

Connor Stratton enjoys learning new things, eating popcorn, and watching movies with friends. He lives in Minnesota.

Table of Contents

Netcare
PHARMACY

nurse

At the Hospital

Many people work at
the hospital.
Nurses work at
the hospital.
They take care of us.

Doctors work at

the hospital.

They learn why we are sick.

They learn why we are hurt.

They know how to help us.

doctor

Checkups

Nurses check our height.
They check our weight.
They check how we
are growing.

Doctors check our hearts.

They check our throats.

They check our health.

Getting Shots and Casts

Nurses give us shots.

They use **needles**.

Shots keep us healthy.

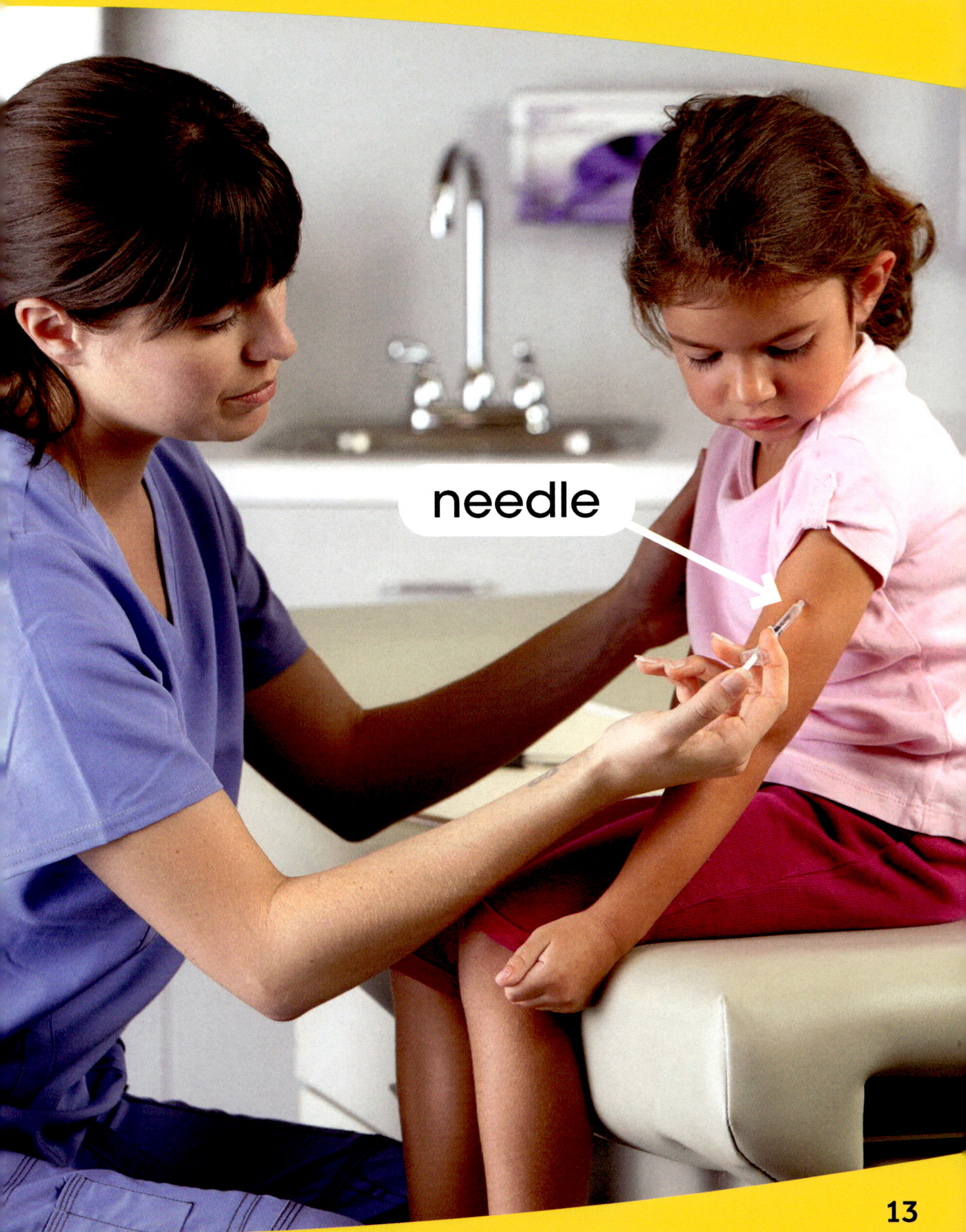
needle

Doctors give us **casts**.

Casts help broken bones.

Casts help bones heal.

cast

Glossary

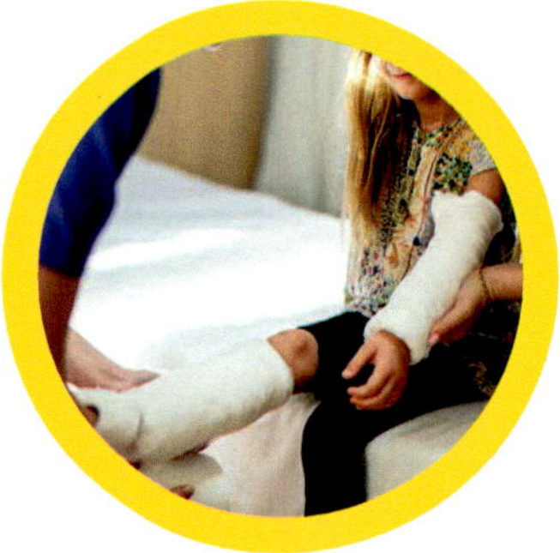

casts

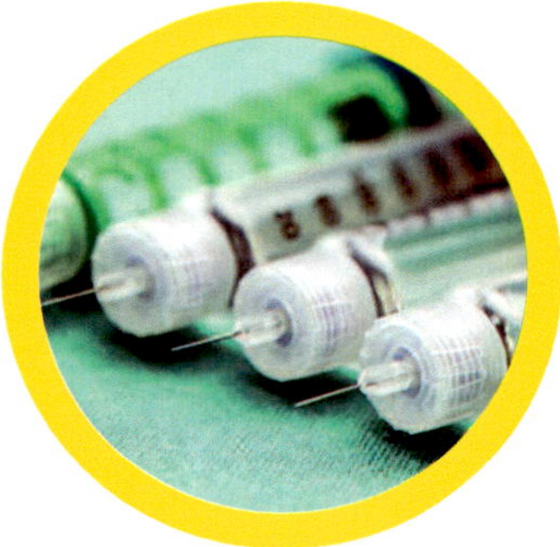

needles

doctors

nurses

Index